Table of Contents

Chapter 1.

I look at my hands, and I see the hardships of work that have taken away the soft boyish palms and replaces them with rough men's fists. I always thought they were powerful hands, yet they could not hold on to the life of the only person I ever truly cared for. As a barbarian, my strength is my only pride. I judge my worth by the battles I have won, by the muscles I have gained, and by the fear I instill. Recently I have learned of a new kind of strength, a muscle I have never known of. A muscle that is more powerful than the strongest steel.

I am Goro, of the Gutian people. Leadership is earned with the honor of blood. In my youth, I served under the great leader Si-um. When I felt I that Si-um was getting gray in the beard and would fail his kills, I challenged him to battle. Si-um fought bravely and with honor, but no man can defeat Goro. I keep the skull of Si-um attached to my bronze shield. Even in death, Si-um watches over his people. Most do not lead for more than five or six years, but I have been the leader of Guti for twelve years. For each life, I place one scar to share their pain and remember their sacrifice which makes me stronger. No man has more scars than Goro, except Erra; God of rage. Our lives are simple, we fight the Akkadians, we take what is theirs until it is gone. Then we move to a new Akkadian land. Should Akkadian's ever best the Guitian people, then they deserve the land more than us. Strength, power, and dominance: these are what is best in life.

The Zagros mountains would shake, the rocks and hills quake in fear when the Gutian people bang their fists against their bronze armor after a battle. I feast on the sacrifices of goats and cattle the Akkadians had set aside for their puny gods. I drink my belly full in wine mixed with the blood of their strongest warriors. Then, I take my pick of their women to keep as my own. Tirigan, the second strongest, he then chooses after me. I can tell that Tirigan wishes to lead, but he does not have the bravery to attack me. I remind him of his place by choosing the women that I know he would want, and making him drink the blood of small children so that we may all laugh at him. After I have had my share of the spoils of battle, I head to my tent to sleep. I am always suspicious that Tirigan will make his attack at night when he thinks I am most vulnerable, but if he is able to best me then he deserves to lead more than I do. Little did I know of the dishonor of cowards. As I slept, Tirigan did indeed approach my tent, but not to attack me as a man does.

The desert was arid and chilling at night, the brown sands danced across the dunes like the enticing but dangerous dance of the asp. This peaceful night was quickly disturbed with the chaotic burst of flames that devoured my tent. With my gut full of the wine of courage, I was slow to move and to understand. The flames licked my face and I felt that I could no longer breathe. Some invisible devil must have been strangling me, and the more I tried to fight him off, the tighter he hung on. In the day, it is not unheard of for the desert to claim a tent with fire, but at night such a thing is unheard of. Before my eyes sealed themselves shut I made out the face of my would-be assassin: Tirigan.

A normal man would be dead after this; and as much as I would like to say that my strength alone protected me, if not for the assistance of an old hermit, this is where my story would end. What occurred next I can only express in the flashes in which they made themselves known to me. This first I opened my eyes, I felt the cold pain of burnt flesh over my whole body. I recognize the remains of my tent, but no other tents surround me. I am left alone, my people have left me to die. In my seclusion and agony, I pray to Erra, but Erra only revels in my pain. I do not pray for safety, for life, or for mercy. I pray for revenge. Tirigan has stolen my honor of dying in battle and dishonors the title of Guiti leader. Again my eyes closed and I feel my life escape my body.

The next moment I wake, I am in a new place. I summon the strength to jump to my feet to defend myself, but my power has left me. I am vulnerable and unable to move at all. For a Guti, this is a fate worse than death. My eyes, in a frenzy, scour the room for answers. I find myself in a small cabin, with tiny furnishings hand made for a tiny person. It is not unlike many of the homes I had destroyed in our raids. However, where people should be, I see nothing but stacks upon stacks of books. Gutians do not read or write, we have no use for books, beyond using them as fire starters when pillaging homes. It is dark out, yet there is something warm and bright about this dwelling. A pleasing odor that I have never smelled before; the smell of leather, which I know all too well, but there is more to the smell. My investigation into my senses was interrupted by the sound of a chair creaking, and a tiny frail man leaning from behind a tower of books. The little old man had a long white beard, and skin as rough and as wrinkled as covers of the book he was holding. He had in his mouth a long wooden pipe, which he only removed to turn pages and mutter to himself. Before I could try to open my mouth to threaten the feeble old man, his eyes looked up to meet mine. For the first time in my life, I had trouble keeping his gaze. "Ah, so you might make it after all." The old man croaked. "Just as well, I'll be wanting my bed back someday."

I had not noticed, but I was lying upon a small bed, my large frame too big. My feet propped up with pillows and chairs. I could not see my body, as it was fully covered in bandages and old animal skins. The pain was a mere echo of what it once was. My eyes again dart to the old man, as if to ask what is wrong with me. Without me muttering a word, the old man answered my question, again looking at his book. "I suspect you cannot move, I also suspect that it'll be a time before you can even talk. When you can speak again, you can call me Enzu. You were pretty badly burned. I had to hitch you to a wagon to drag you here. You're the first person to visit my home for in...oh...many years." His voice starts to travel off, as if he were starting to talk more to himself than to me, at that point. "Hopefully you'll be the last to visit. I don't need the bother." My eyes slowly close on their own again.

For the next few months, I rested, when I did awake the little old man would speak. Sometimes to me, and sometimes a mumble to himself. I've never had one person share the conversation, without another person speaking. Sometimes he would tell me stories, stories about places far away. He would stare at his books, and then tell me about kings and countries, he would tell me about the stars and about creatures that live in vast oceans. It was as if, as long as he was looking at one of these books, he would never run out of things to say. It was during one of these storied sessions that something caught my attention. "Despite its monstrous size, the blue whale cannot swallow anything much larger than a grapefruit." The old man then started to ramble about the various sizes a grapefruit can be. I felt a tingle in my lips as the muscles started to quiver and I heard my voice ask; "Why?" "Hmm? Eh? What's that? Did I just hear the most important question in the world? Ha Ha!", Enzu cackled. "You wait this long to speak, you get only one word to be your first, and you choose a remarkable one! Well, you see it has to do with blue whales anatomy." Again, the old man understood me without me saying another word, because he could see the confusion in my eyes. "Anatomy, it's the study of a human or animal's body." Again, my confusion clouded over my eyes. "How do you know so many things?" I ask the old man. "The books!", the old man shouts, breaking the peace in a way that makes my heart muscle stop. "The books tell me everything." I could not hear the books, I assume it was because the old man was talking over them.

A few weeks later, I had enough strength in me to sit up, move my arms, to hold my own food, and to speak as I once did. "Let me hear from the books", I request. Enzu gave me an odd look but handed me one of the books. I opened it, just as he does, I turned some pages, as Enzu does, but I heard nothing. There was nothing but little scribbles in each book, no pictures or anything that I could understand. I watched the old man, he squinted deep at each book. Aha, a look that I recognize! Many warriors I have seen give this serious and aggressive look to captured enemies, to find out information about those that we fight in battle. *Somehow this tiny frail man has intimidated his books into telling him information.* I ask the old man if any of the books teach him about battle, war, or killing. "When I was young,"Enzu said hesitantly, "I read about tactical affairs, but long ago I decided to live a life of a pacifist." Many times the old man used words that were strange to me, but given that this was a word of war, I felt I must ask for clarity. "What form of fighting style is this 'pass-a-fist'? I shall learn it, and master it." I said confidently. Enzu just laughed to himself and went on reading. No man has ever laughed at me and survived, but I liked this old man.

Enzu at his books, and they told him about what herbs I needed to ease my pain. He would leave, sometimes for many hours, searching the wilderness for each herb. From time to time he would find a jar with only a few plants in it, he would hesitate and then mutter "He needs it more than you, stick to the plan. Your pain will end soon, his is only starting" I assumed he was speaking to the books, but I don't understand what books would need with plants. The most recent time he looked at me and smiled. "I've made you a pipe, so that you can smoke as well, as we read." he said, as he handed me a long wooden pipe. I did not like any fire so close to my face, but I held it in my mouth anyway. The old man slowly poured himself into his chair like a glob of mud. He seemed to struggle more and more with getting around. Once he was finally settled in, he lit up his pipe and started to tell me what the books were saying to him. "The Black Panther is a big cat (of any species, but most commonly a jaguar or a leopard) whose coloration is entirely black. This may have originated from the

Latin name 'Panthera' and was probably shortened from Black Panthera to Black Panther." All the while he was speaking, he pointed his pipe around in time with his words. As he looked up from the pages, he found that I too was swinging my pipe around along with his words. His brow curled up, as he then looked at his own pipe. Our eyes made contact and we both let out a long and hearty laugh. For the first time in my life, I was not killing, I was not celebrating a kill, I was just enjoying the company of another person.

I asked many questions, something
I had never done before. Guitians look to
me for answers, not for questions. Enzu
taught me that the books tell him to ask
questions and to listen more than speaking;
this is how we become great leaders. It
was while asking questions that I learned of
the old man's history, and learned the
meaning of a word I had heard shouted at
me from my enemies, but never

understood: mercy. "I came here, long long ago," the old man told me, "from the East. Before all of this was a barbarian country, when it was all green and fruit trees. When the Tigris river was full of life and beauty. I came with my people, to start a new life. I built the whole town. I ran the library, I had more books then. than I do now, if you can believe that. We weren't a large tribe, but we were very happy. A group of barbarians from the Zagros mountains came down, like a clap of thunder. They took my wife, they killed the men, and they set fire to our homes. These leather-bound books, these were my only armor. As the town around me burned to the ground, I laid in a cocoon of books, protecting me from the outside flames. A page burns easy, but a leather-bound book does not so easily catch fire. The outside pages burn, but I stayed safe deep under a pile. Those brainless barbarians assumed I was dead. If they had stayed even a few moments later, the books would have burned through and I would have been gone. I did escape, though. I built me this cabin, I stay away from the barbarian people, with their fighting and bloodshed. I find burned down villages, like my own, and I gather any remaining books. I look after them, I learn from them. I suppose it's my thank you for saving my life. Imagine my surprise" he says with a small chuckle, "to see you. A half-burned book as big as a horse." My heart muscle felt heavy, as I knew it was my people that destroyed his family. I wanted to make things right, but I lacked the words to ask for forgiveness. My life had always been focused on my own strength, my own survival, and my own desires. I had never thought about the people we challenged.

With this shame, I struggled to find the
words, but I asked him: "You must hate the
men that have done this to you. You must
want to kill all those that have taken from
you." The old man looked up from his
book again, but not at me. Instead, he
looks directly into the fireplace and says, in
a soft voice; "I did. I did hate them, but
now I pity them. They will never have
peace, they will never know joy. Their life
is empty, that is their punishment. That is
my revenge. I wish them all a long life."
He then closed his book, leaned back, and
slept.

Eventually, my strength returned to
me, the pain had gone away. Upon removing
the bandages and animal skins, I have found
that my skin is crumpled like the pages of the
old man's books. It is dark and many colors,
it is no longer tan and rough. I also notice that

my battle scars have all faded away. Perhaps I am a new man, with my new skin. I go to find Enzu, to ask him what the books say about my scars, but he has not woken up. It is strange to see the old man asleep in the middle of the day. At this time he would be talking to his books while cooking a stew or lighting his pipe while looking for a book about some ancient religion. With my newfound strength, I jovially pick up Enzu, still in his chair, and hoist him above my head. "You don't even recognize me, do you old man?" I say with a loud guffaw. But he barely stirred at all. My heart muscle, again felt heavy, as I knew something was very wrong. "Enzu!" I exclaimed. "What is wrong?" The old man wheezed and sputtered but softly stated: "I am, as you say, an old man. I knew my time was soon. Take care of my friends." He motioned slightly to the piles of books around him. "And take care of yourself...my friend." I knew our time was short, and I had little chance to express my sorrow for losing him and for what my people had done to him. I started to explain who I was and who my people were, but the old man gave out a laugh which turned into coughs, as he stated: "I know, I knew when I saved you. How many villagers wear full bronze armor to sleep?" The blood in my veins turned to ice, as I asked; "Then why did you save me?" Enzu paused for a moment, and he said in a timid voice: "I wanted you all to live a long life, that is my revenge. Goro, I saved you for the wrong reasons. I did hate you, I hated all barbarians when I saved you. You are not a barbarian, though. You are just another book. The barbarians did not see your value, so they burned you. I rescued you, and you taught me many things." "NO!" I yelled to Enzu, as I jumped to my feet. "I learn from you, you taught me, you made me a different man. I understand now that there is more to life than violence and rage, more than drinking and taking. I understand now what pacifist means. I was a man of hate and rage, and you taught me to care about others." Enzu smiled for the first time, but still would not look at me, and he said "I was not a violent man on the outside, but I was a man of hate and rage as well, and it was you that taught me to care about others again. I still wish a long life for you, but only because you are a more complete man now." Enzu closed his eyes for the long sleep. I call out for the old man, but he does not open his eyes. I shake him slightly, but he will not wake. I feel the frenzy that I have only ever felt in battle, my heart beats fast, my mind races. I shout at him. "You cannot be dead! You are a man of peace!" In my lifetime, all men that die, die in battle. I had never before endured the loss of anyone from old age. I frantically pick up

book after book, I stare at them as the old man
did. I scream, I curse, I threaten, but nothing I
can do will intimidate the books into telling
me how to wake my only friend. I pray to
Nabu, Thoth, Enki, Mergden and all of the
gods that the old man read to me about, but
none will listen to me. My journey is clear; I
must earn the respect of the books, so that
they will share with me the wisdom of how to
bring the old man back to me.

Chapter 2.

I lay Enzu in his bed to bring him
comfort for the long sleep. I exhaust myself

intimidating each book until I drift off to
sleep in the old man's chair.

I awake in a dark and cold building. The rough
stone scratches my charred skin. I jump to my feet,
unclear how I got to where I am. A small light
appears in front of me and grows brighter and larger.
The light becomes so bright that I must shield my eyes
from burning, and I am reminded of the betrayal that
altered my flesh. As quickly as the light approached, it
snuck away again. In its place, stands a dozen stone
thrones, each with a great Guitian leader sitting upon
it. I stand at the heel of Si-Um, the leader I brought to
glory in death. Si-Um seems larger than when he was
alive, even while seated upon a throne his stature is
that of a grand mountain. He resembles a massive
beast, more than the man I served. His eyes scan the
horizon and do not seem to notice me.

For the first time in my memory, I feel like an
ant when standing before another man. "Si-Um!" I

shout up to the sitting mountain, but he does not move.
I start to question if he is just a grand statue and not
the Si-Um I knew. Once I was quite certain that this
was not the real Si-Um, a thundering boom shook the
ground around me and I heard the voice of my former
leader. "Goro, where are your people?" I looked
closely at the face, but it still did not move, yet the
sound was clearly coming from the being on the stone
chair. "My people?" I inquire back, feelings of rage
start stirring in my bones. "Tirigan has taken my
people. He has not battled me and earned his right as a
leader. My people have left me to die without honor. "
I shout back. No sooner than I finish the last word,
another booming voice comes, now from an older
leader, from before my time. "You seek our help,
then?" I think for a moment, something I would never
have done before meeting the old man. "Yes. If you
can help, I will accept it." The ground shakes as
Si-Um bellows to me; "You want revenge? You wish
to lead your people once again. We can help." I bark
back to the voice "No. My people left me to die

without honor. I have no people. I do want revenge, but I will learn to let that feeling go. Enzu saved me, how do I save him? How do I bring him back to me? You live on after death, teach me. Teach me to give the old man the power to speak to me in dreams, as you do!"

The ground shakes more violently than before, as a legion of voices shout at me. The sound is so strong I must cover my ears to keep my skull from shaking out. What bit I could understand from the voices were angry. "Only in battle is a man immortalized!" "There is no glory in his death!" "Our secrets are not for the timid!" With all the strength I possess I plead with the elders as loud as I can "Quiet!" Silence fills the stone structures. Si-Um again speaks to me. "Look behind you, Goro." As I turn, I see an empty stone throne. "This is the throne for the next in our line. This was to be your throne, but we question the direction you traveling in life. Your new path will lead you away from this throne."

24

Without a second thought, I call out "Give the throne to Enzu. I will give up my throne for him!" Once more the ground moves like ocean waves and the voices create tremors in my skull. Each elder shouting curses and threats. I cry out for them to stop, over and over I beg, but they will not listen. Then, when my pain feels so strong that I worry I cannot survive it, I awaken. Again, I am in Enzu's cottage.

I have spoken to each of these books, I have done every form of torture I know, I have begged and pleaded, yet these books will not tell me how to save the old man. My sleep vision has taught me that the dead can be made immortal. Though my ancestors have the secrets, they would not help me. I spat at their memory and decided to travel on, searching for the secret myself. I told the old man of my plans, though I knew he could hear me. I left behind my weapons and my armor. The old man has shown me that such things weigh down my mind more than my body. I took enough food to carry with me but left enough for

Enzu. I knew he would be hungry when I brought him back from the long sleep. Enzu said he came from the east, so that is the direction I went.

I followed the Tigris river so that I always had fresh water. From time to time I came across a traveling merchant or an outlying tribe of nomads. They saw my discolored and papered skin, and they kept their distance. For this reason, I decided to create a cloak to hide my unusual appearance. I left the river path and traveled deep into the wilderness to gather leaves and tall grass. As I grabbed the trunk of a tree, to uproot it and gather the larger leaves that grow upon the top, a dark shadow moves above my head. I slowly let go of the trunk and took a few steps back. This shadow was not created by the sun, this shadow moves of its own will. Unlike shadows I have seen of the past, this shadow had glowing, green eyes. It moved like a lion, with no fear, yet it was more agile. It jumped from branch to branch as sure-footed as if it were on solid ground. My mind had another vision, a

26

shorter vision, one of the old man's stories. This was
no shadow, this was a panther.

It's glassy, jaded eyes were fixed on me and
me alone. It remained low, as if ready to pounce at any
moment. I reached for my ax and felt nothing but air.
The quick movement of my hand persuaded the beast
to leave its perch and leap towards me in the attack.
With all the strength in my legs, I rolled out of the
way. Now the panther and I circled each other, there
was no question, one of us would have to die this
night. The large cat let out a cry, with a sound I have
never heard before. Without reacting I yelled back at
the creature, showing it no fear. "I am a man of peace,
I have no interest in fighting you!" I plead with the
beast, though it shows no interest in my words.
Instead, it swipes its massive claws into my chest. I
feel it's power overwhelm me. It carries with it no
fear, but also no joy in attacking me. This is no sport,
it is survival. It leaps at me again, this time I grab
onto the panther. I feel its muscles strain against my

own. The panther is not afraid to kill, but he does not kill for fun. He protects himself, he kills to eat or to keep from being eaten. I can be a man of non-violence, and still, protect myself from danger. As I squeezed the animal tighter and felt the life struggle less and less, I felt regret that such a majestic being must die. There was no glory in the killing, but there is no glory in death either. Though I know the panther cannot understand my words, I cannot help but say "Thank you for the lesson you have taught me. I will make your death mean something, you will not have died for nothing." No sooner than I speak these words, the large beast goes limp. I have taken the life of a giant beast with my bare hands, a feat that I would have been proud of earlier in life.

I pull out the largest tooth from the beasts jaw and fashion a knife from it. I skin the panther, quite easily and make a robe. The dark fur almost blends into the black and purple skin I now have. I cannot help but compare myself to the Panther again. I look to the face of the beast and say: "I will wear you always, you will be a part of me. I will take your knowledge with me." I then place the panther skin over my own, its face covers my head. As my bronze armor defined myself as a warrior in my past, so to will this fur define me as a peaceful man, which I am working to become. I will only bring harm to others if I must to survive. My knife is my panther's tooth, it will continue to only taste blood if no other option presents itself.

Chapter 3

As I travel back to the Tigris river path, people no longer wince in fear, because my disfigurements are covered by my new panther fur. Still, I feel unrest. In battle, a clear and obvious task lays ahead of me: to attack. My new path was less structured. However, the trail I walked eventually became a road, and what was once a few merchants passing by, became buildings and homes. As I enter the village I wonder "what business do I have in entering the kind of place I have done so much to harm?" If at any moment my feet wanted to turn away and walk out of the town, I looked at my fur and reminded myself that I am a new man. By the time I have walked halfway into the town, I heard a familiar sound; the rhythmic marching of armor. Before my mind could react, my feet changed their course to follow the hypnotic sound. What I saw was not an army, but instead, a series of old farmers and young men covered in loose-fitting metal, carrying crude and unsharpened weapons. These men were not on their way to battle, they were on their way to be slaughtered. A small welp of a boy, dragging a sword behind him, came rushing behind me. I could not hold in my laugh when I saw him trip over his own feet, trying to keep up with the rest of the would-be fighters. "Boy!" I called out, making him jump nearly out of his bronze chest piece. "Where is this rabble headed? Why do you march to your deaths?" I ask. The boy takes a deep breath as he tries to fake a sense of courage in his words. "An army, much larger and much better equipped have come to destroy our homes. We will meet them in battle and protect our families, and I am no boy. I am Shul-pa-e, the last of my family line." I wrinkle my brow at the boy, in the same way, the old man would do to me when I said something that seemed incorrect to him. "Nonsense!" I shout to him, making the whole of the marchers stop in their tracks and turn to me. "There is no glory in dying. This is the lesson I have recently discovered. Do not go out and die needlessly, it will not protect your village." A dusty old farmer, lame in both eyes, shouts in my direction; "Then what would you have us do? You are right, there is no glory in dying, but there is no glory in giving up either. You look like you've seen battle. Tell us what to do. Lead us, and we will be in your favor!"

No sooner than he finished his words, the whole procession peaked up. A sense of hope swept across the crowd. Each man stood a bit taller, their faces seemed a bit brighter, and they stood upon the ends of their feet waiting to hear my reply. "I-I cannot." I sputtered out. "I am a man of peace now. I will not kill unless it is to protect myself." I was surprised to find that I was more disappointed by my reply than the crowd in front of me. I know that killing is wrong, but my whole life was defined by victory in battle. "Then don't fight." The blind man yells back. This idea hits me so powerful, that I must take a step back to remain on my feet. "Teach us how to survive an attack." He yells to me.

      I never thought of myself as a teacher. I never thought that my experience could be used for good. Yet here I am, walking through the town, shouting out orders. "Douse that roof with water, that thatch will be an easy target for fire! Get these horses indoors, they will attract attention! Keep that water boiling, when you see the first wave approach the gate, you'll need it hot to burn any siege-masters, and the steam will give you cover against arrows!" I felt a rush in my blood I have not felt in a long time. I leaned against the crude sandstone bricks of the main gate, with the young soldier at my side, each of the defenses of the town lined up hidden behind the stones. The sound of trumpets sound and we can feel the ground tremble with the clacking of hooves grow closer. Shul-pa-e comes scurrying towards me with the look of a child sneaking up on its siblings. "I have fashioned a bow, I will be a great warrior like you once were." Before I can protest his desire for violence, he sits up and fires an arrow at the enemy attackers. I reach up and grab the young welp by the shirt and slam him back down beside me. The end result is an arrow that fires almost straight up in the air and lands near his own leg. "Stay down! All of you! This is only the scouts, not the army. Let them find a defenseless town, they will go back and the raiders will expect an easy victory. Don't let them know our plan before we get to put it into action!" The young man looking ashamed, but when he sees no judgment in my eyes, he goes back to his focus. I had to stifle my own laughter when I noticed that Shul-pa-e only had one arrow.

We heard the horses traveled through the gates, into the village. We saw a few small fires lit, some shouting in a Babylonian dialect I was not familiar with, and sure enough, the riders leave back the way they came. I instruct a few men to keep the fire from spreading but to be sure not to put the fires out. "We don't want to raise any suspicion. Let them think we are in a panic. Make our weakness our strength." No more than a few moments passed, but I could tell on their faces that it seemed like a lifetime to the villagers. The sound of drums and horns sound and the roar of well-trained soldiers pierce the peacefulness of the village. I lean one eye over the gate to assess the army, and each villager does the same. A small army runs towards us, enough that a handful of barbarian fighters could hold off, easily. I smile knowing that victory is at hand, but my smile is robbed of me as I am reminded that these are no barbarian fighters. These are scared villagers that have never fought a day in their lives. "By the plow of Dagon!" The villagers muttered. "There are more soldiers than I ever imagined!" I speak in a low, but solid voice; "Hold true. We have the element of surprise. That fear you feel now, we will give to them. They will never stand against you again. This village will be famous for its battle. There IS glory in what we do today!”

My eyes travel back to the running soldiers headed our way. “Look now!” I shout to the villagers. The front line of the army, men with large clubs and flails, running and snorting like wild bulls, all come crashing down. What they thought was yet another dune, was actually a trench dug with villagers own farming tools, and filled with wet and muddy sand. The speed and power that the fighters prided themselves in, was used against them. Their shins and legs snapped under their own weight, and they tripped up the runners behind them. A title wave of warriors came to a halt, which spread a ripple of fear throughout the entire army.

As the next wave of men, with their curved swords and their round wooden shields, cautiously made their way closer to the village, a flock of spears made from the sharpened ends of rakes and shovels descended upon the attackers. The flimsy shields, designed to protect against arrows, splintered under the force of the spears. Leaving the warriors defenseless and afraid. Many of the "brave soldiers" ran back to the safety of the remaining army. The final group, the men with long-swords on horseback zig-zagged their way around the bodies left behind. They traveled all the way to the sandy gate, dismounted and started to chip away at the wooden door of the gatehouse. The villagers poured their pots of boiling water on the first few. The steam mixed with melting flesh to create a pink mist that engulfed the men. While the second wave of villagers tossed clay pots of fire and oil onto the remaining fighters, screams of panic and horror echoed through the land. The military generals and leaders who were watching the battle from a distance saw only a cloud of vapor and flashing light. It was as if the village was defended by Ishkur; God of storms and thunder. The generals motioned for the trumpet of retreat, but no warriors survived to come back, only a few frightened horses ran from the cloudy carnage. The villagers cheer their victory, and each shouts over the other just how thankful they are to me for saving them.

That night we celebrate our decisive victory with wine, dancing, and a feast. Unlike my usual post-battle celebration, I am being offered grapes, veal, ale, and other delicious and rare things I do not have to take for myself. Others sing my praise, I do not sing my praise to others. One compliment stands above all others; Shul-pa-e runs to me with a cup spilling over with wine and jovially expresses: "All praise to Goro, the smartest man in the village!" I have been called many things, and claimed many more, but never have I been called smart. Never have I thought of myself as smart. I knock the drink from the young man's hand and shout; "You have let the drink go to your head. Do not confuse my compassion for weakness, I will not tolerate you mocking me!" Shul-pa-e's smile escapes from his face but quickly returns as he laughs again. "Goro, you alone knew

every step that the warriors were going to make
against us. You taught us to use our strengths to save
ourselves. If any other attackers come to us again, we
will know how to survive. It was your thoughts that
saved us all." I contemplate these words as I leave the
celebration behind.

I walk the dark streets of the village alone, to
let these thoughts settle within me. Every so often a
young couple run past holding hands, or a child dances
across the alleys, excited to be awake so late in the
evening. In my deep thought, I ignored the sound of
feet having run towards me, and almost jumped when
the young man touches my shoulder. "Goro, have I
upset you?" He says, in a much more sober and
somber voice. I tell the Shul-pa-e about the books,
and my quest to earn their respect. He seems
confused, but he keeps his questions to himself.
"Learn all that you can. Listen closely to the old blind
farmer, he has so much to teach you." I express to the
young man. "Elam-nu?" The young man asks.

"Nobody listens to old men, but I've often heard him talk about how life used to be. I have ideas on how to use his old farming ways to improve our grains, but who will listen to a young boy and an old man?" I think before I speak, and reply. "If they do not listen, do it anyway. If you fail, you will look no more foolish, and if you do not fail, you will have proven your worth. Where is the risk in that?" Shul-pae-e's eyes become deep in thought, and with that, I left him so that we may both reflect more on what each of us has said.

The next day, I make my way to the village gates to continue my travels. The entire village stands to the sides of the main street and tosses flowers in my path. At first, I am confused by the gesture and was hesitant to move forward, eventually, I understood them doing what they saw as respect. I honored them by accepting their gestures. Shul-pa-e and Elam-nu stand on either side of the main gate, blocking my path. Without words I stopped in front of them, waiting to hear why they have blocked my path. Shul-pa-e has with him something familiar, something that makes my eyes widen. He has a leather-bound book, one that I have never seen before. "What is this? Where did you find this?" I ask in a stern voice. Shul-pa-e looks to Elam-nu, then back to me. "We made this for you. It is your story." My eyes squinted at the cover, then they traveled back to the face of the young man. The look of confusion seemed clear, as he tried to explain further. "Um, look here." He points to the cover of the book, where a few squiggly lines were carved into the leather. "The mind of steel, that's you. The pages are blank, you can add to it your story." I take the book, though I still do not understand what it is. Books keep their secrets, but this book hides them more than others. This must be the most important secret of all. This must be the book that carries with it the power to give immortality to Enzu. I had the book, I had a secret, now I needed to take the secret from the book.

Chapter 4

I head farther east, the sun and the moon being my only companions. Each day I open the book with no words, and I shout. I threaten. I refuse it food. I raise my fists to attack. Nothing I do seems to phase the book, it keeps its secrets from me. Eventually, the sands and shrubs transform into lush grass and trees. Such oasis' are the settings for towns, but this area continues on without people or buildings. This was no oasis, this was a new land. This must be the land of Enzu. Finally, my journey will come to an end.

As the sun fell into a slumber and the moon was making its way to watch over the earth, I noticed an object over the horizon. Though not very large, it was very out of place. A tent, just big enough to fit a few men inside was pitched by itself. Next to it a glowing fire and a spit with a roasted boar shimmering in the camp light. The insects and birds continued their songs, not afraid of whatever was hidden inside of the tent. " *If they find no danger, then neither should I.* " I reasoned.

As I walked confidently towards the tent, my foot snapped a twig under its weight. The flaps of the tent blossom, and out steps an unfamiliar site. Before me stood a young woman, covered head to toe in bright-colored scarves and silks. Her skin was as dark as the night sky behind her, painted black with gold dots over each eye. She moved with the grace of a leaf on a deep pond. She seemed unaffected by my presence, even after having looked at me right in my face. She moved around me, almost gliding across the grass.

My mind was filled with questions, but a new question came to mind before I could finish the last one, which kept me from making any noise at all. The stagnant silence ceased by the woman's soft tones. "Why am I here? That is the first question you want to ask." I was stunned by her understanding of my thoughts. "Yes, I suppose it is." I manage to stutter out. "Perhaps I came here to meet you. Or perhaps that is why you came here. To meet me." Unsatisfied with her answer I open my mouth to speak again, but she softly interrupts me, still not showing any focus on me. "Who am I? The next question of yours." I take a moment to collect my thoughts, frightened by her ability to read my words before I speak them. She answers her own question with: "I am a priestess of Nisaba; Goddess of grain and scribal knowledge." The grain is a subject I vaguely understand, many of the villages I have attacked, and the village I have most recently saved both grew grain. Scribal knowledge is a phrase I was less familiar with. I understand knowledge though. "Knowledge? Yes. I have need of knowledge, but when I pray to Gods of knowledge they do not listen. My words fall into silence." The priestess looked at me with her gold painted eyes, and I felt as though they were sharp knives stabbing through my skin and looking into my mind itself. "You shout to the Gods and expect shouts back. You must learn to speak softly and listen loudly. Ask me softly about what you want. But be warned, I will only be here for this one night, so think carefully about what you want me to say on your behalf. What one thing do you want to know about anything else." She then gracefully tucked herself back into her tent.

Again, I sat alone with only the moon looking down at me.

I think until my thoughts run together into dreams, I feel my eyes glaze as the fire in front of me becomes just a hazy glow. My mind was unaware that my body had fallen asleep, so it kept on seeing the world around me. I saw the stars above, the little holes in the panther fur of the sky. They danced around and changed places in the sky. Before long they merged together and became two wolves, one larger and one smaller. They circle each other, ready to fight. The smaller wolf was aggressive and quick to fight, while the larger one was docile and gentle. The smaller made growls and bit repeatedly at the larger one, which just looked on like a tired mother watching her cubs play. After a time, the larger one let out a single bark, which frightened the smaller wolf away. Before I could decipher what had happened to me, I shook awake.

Sunrise was almost upon me, I had to ask a question right away, or lose out on this chance.

I step towards the tent again. Once more, the flaps of the tent lift themselves and the woman flow out of her tent like a silent river. "Which questions do you have, fellow traveler and seeker of knowledge?" She asks, in a voice as soft and as dark as the panther fur I wear. I attempt to speak softly and slowly, but still, sound powerful. The result was me pushing the words from the deeper parts of my throat, sounding more like a croaking toad. The priestess's eyes widen at the unpleasant sound. "Where do I go to find the lessons I need to learn?" The priestess hesitates, as she reflects on the noise from me. "Where are your people, Goro?" The woman asks. A familiar question, which distracted me from noticing that the priestess knew my name. "I have no people, they have left me to die," I repeat back to her. "Go to them, show them your strength. Not with force, but with forgiveness. Show them that you keep control over your thoughts and emotions, not them." I reflect on the priestess' words. "If I see Tirigan again, he will die by my hand or me by his. Even if I don't attack him right away, surely he will attack me. Gutians will follow their commands, if Tirigan tells them to kill me, I will defend myself. Who am I against an army of warriors?" The priestess looks away from me again and goes back to ignoring my presence. "Tirigan is not the leader." She says softly. "I am not a leader. I will never lead again." I say sternly. "You will not." The priestess agrees, which turned my spine to stone. "If you want to find the true leader, look for the mother."

Chapter 5

Traveling forward, just to head back to the Zagros mountains, seemed like a wasted journey. But the priestess was the only one of Enzo's people I could find. If she is half as learned as he, then I would be right to follow her advice.

As I travel back I think upon her words "look for the mother", and I think about my own mother. Natural born Gutian women are very rare. Once men get strong enough to swing a weapon, they become warriors. They travel on raids and take the women of their choosing. Once those women give the man a son, she is set back to the Zagros mountains to raise him until he is old enough to carry a weapon, and likely he will never see her again. If the child she bears is a girl, the child is left behind to die. Sometimes a leader will show favor upon a young girl, often his own, and they are permitted to be raised in the mountains. Only those can ever be truly married to another Gutian. Though being married to a warrior that never comes home, is not as prestigious as they would have you believe. As Gutian warriors have a ranking based on strength and skill, so do the women have a ranking based on blood purity. Those born with two Gutian parents, as viewed as real Gutians, the rest are just property. Though if you ask any Gutian man, all women are his property. His weapon, his horse, and his women are his property, and often valued in that order.

My own mother was not pure Gutian. The last I
ever saw her was when I was only a child. Another
vision laid over my eyes, different than the others.
The lush greenery around me faded into a rocky brown
mountain path. The cold air stung my skin like a
thousand tiny scorpions. I looked down at my hands,
and what was once bulky man's fists are once again a
tiny boy's grasp. The darkness is held back by
numerous torches surrounding a legion of small huts. I
frantically glanced around me, alone and afraid, but no
sooner than the panic enters does it leave once again as
familiar arms wrap around my miniature shoulders. I
spin around and lock eyes with the most comforting
and gentle eyes I will ever see. One look scares away
the cold, and I feel as if I am covered in blankets and
placed in front of a fire. "Goro." My mother said, in a
soft and sweet voice. "Go back to bed, you will freeze
out here." Her arms hold my shoulders as she leads me
back to our hut. Once inside the hut, my mother
handed me a bowl and poured it in a warm stew. No
food has ever tasted as good. My vision goes hazy as

if looking through the heat of a fire. My bowl dropped from my lap and spills to the floor. I hear the sound of horses galloping in front of the hut, and a very large man stands on the threshold. His eyes filled with ice and hollow as a barren cave. Without words, he thrusts his arm out and grabbed me by the shoulder. I winced in pain and in my fear I looked to my mother, who avoids eye contact. I call out to her and hear no echo of a reply. Her head sank to the floor as her back turned towards me. "It is your time, Goro. You must learn what it is to be a man now." She can barely speak her words, holding in tears and trying to stay strong.

Her words clatter around in my ears as the vision fades and I am once more traveling the road as a grown man. My mother's face is obscured from me, only her eyes stand out. *How will I find my mother, if I only recall her eyes?* I ask myself. Still, my destination is clear, even if my quest is not. The mountains are much closer than Enzu's cabin and require a different path than the river I had been following. *It won't be much longer*, I think as I glance at the mysterious book. It wasn't more than a few night's journeys before I saw the Great Zab river, a familiar sight from my childhood.

The aggressive waters flow down like war horses, flooding the ground as well as my ears. I feel the calm of war, as well as the calm of peace in this sound. No sooner than I revel in this new feeling, I was startled back into reality by movement in the distance. I nearly dropped my belongings as I instinctively reached for a phantom weapon. Remembering my new path of peace, I cautiously moved closer. *Gutians are unlikely to be back home this time of year, however, I cannot be too careful.* I reasoned to myself. As I approached the moving stranger, my body refused to continue on. My muscles locked into place. Before me stood a woman, a Gutian woman for certain. Her pale skin and light hair were unmistakable. However, what really stood out to me was her eyes. As she turned away from the clothes she was washing in the river, I saw before me two bright green eyes that fill me with warmth. This woman was too young to be my mother, yet no other eyes have ever had such an effect.

With a shaky voice of a small child, I cried out "Mother?" The reply back sent ice down my spine. "Yes? Who calls for me?" I fall to my knees and weep. I don't understand how this woman could be my mother, but for a single moment, I was again a weak little boy. Ready to pick up my life, where it left off all those years ago. "Do I know you, stranger?" Asked the woman, if a firm but gentle voice. "It is me, Goro! Mother, I have come home! Tell me you remember me?!" I express, showing emotions reserved only for children and not befitting of Gutian warriors. "Goro?!" She exclaimed in a shocked and confused voice. "I have heard of you, yes. But I was told you died. I think you are mistaken though, we have never met." My mind is overwhelmed, what was once a comforting sound of the river is now a hammer banging against my ears. "You are not my mother? Yet you answered to me as Mother? What trickery is this? What evil-" Before I could finish my tirade of fierce questions, the woman laughs softly. This gentle sound disarms my anger, and she explains. "How could I be your mother? I am, if anything, younger than you? I answer to Mother, for that is what our people call me. I am the mother of the Gutian tribe. The mother of knowledge. The wife of Tirigan, the man that claims to have bested you in battle. Though despite your many scars, you do not seem very dead and your scars are not that of battle."

"What mother of knowledge are you, to give yourself to a man like Tirigan. He is a coward and not fit to sit upon the ancients thrown. He is no leader." I bark at the woman, turning my face away from her eyes. Though I could not see her, I could hear a smile across her face. "And you would come back to become a leader again? To take your revenge and your place as leader of the Gutian people, is that your plan?" My eyes slowly turn back to the woman. " No. I am no longer Gutian. I will never lead again." The woman raises her eyebrows as she speaks; "So what do you care if he leads or does not? They aren't your people any longer. Let them suffer." My eyes widen. I had not considered this. "I am Nawaritum." The woman says, leaving me to dwell upon her question. "Come with me to the mountains. I'm sure my husband will be...happy to hear that you survived his battle."

"Why is Tirigan here in the mountains? Why is he not at war, as is a tradition for the Gutians?" I ask Nawaritum, as we travel up the mountain. "Tirigan has little stomach for a real battle, as you know. He is content to attack small villages and then travel back to the mountains before anyone can pick up a weapon against him. He stays here in the mountains like a child, and does not travel the warpath, as you once did." I notice a familiar tone in her voice. "You seem to share a dislike of your husband, as I do. Am I wrong?" Nawaritum smiles again. "You were correct before, a mother of knowledge would never give herself willingly to a man like Tirigan. But, as you know, when he became the leader he had the right to choose his own wife. What he did not know, is that as a learned woman, I know how to gain the rewards of being a leader's wife, while staying out of the leader's bed. A woman of knowledge would never give herself to a man like Tirigan. Still, he is the Gutian leader. Even if you will not kill Tirigan, I'm sure when the people learn of your return they will turn on him."

I stop walking and look up at the sun and the passing of time. "Do not tell them who I am, then. I am not here for revenge. I wish Tirigan a long life, this is my revenge." Nawaritum also stopped walking, turned back to me and said: "Spoken like a truly learned man."

Chapter 6

As I make my way through the village, each woman and each small child turn their face from me while keeping their eyes fixed on mine. They were not accustomed to strangers in their home, as I am not accustomed to being a stranger to faces that I know well. Deep in the mountains, with a fortress of rock on all sides, the Gutian women and children are protected from danger. Yet, in the farthest area, I see a building that is new to me. A large pale stone fortress seems to have erupted from the mountain itself. In his brick cacoon, I find the coward Tirigon hiding like a small child, wrapped in his mother's skirt. His eyes narrow upon seeing me, and I turn my eyes away, worried that he would recognize the anger I keep hidden away.

"Nawaritum." He says, addressing his queen, though his eyes do not leave my face. "Who is this eye-sore of a man you bring before me? Some surviving farmer that comes seeking revenge from a raid? A father came to tell off his daughter's captor? No, this man seems strong enough to battle and yet stands peaceful and silent. Guards! Remove this man's weapons." Two large men unveil themselves from the shadows behind Tirigan. As they approach, I quickly reach for my book, which causes them both to

draw weapons. "Do not bother," I say in a gentle
voice. "My only weapon is knowledge, do not be
deceived by outward appearance, I am but a humble
scholar, wishing to write the legacy of Tirigan the
brave." The words stick in my throat like heavy
molasses, yet I somehow manage to get them out.

A look of pure joy and wonder flows over the
face of Tirigan. "Splendid! You will write the story of
my most splendid victory! I will finally put an end to
the war against all Arkadians!" The two guards lower
their weapons and look upon Tirgan in disbelief as he
openly shares secrets with a complete stranger. "Do
not look upon me as a fool! I tell you, I know how to
read men better than your queen or this scholar can
read books. I trust this man as hardily as I would trust
Nawaritum herself." Upon hearing this Nawaritum
and I share a knowing glance. "Tell me, stranger,
what shall I call you?" Without thinking I stand tall to
introduce myself. "My name is Gor-" before I finish
Nawaritum makes a quick gasp and cough, to remind

me not to use my real name. Thinking quickly I finish. "....bage." Tirigan looks at me slightly less impressed. "Your name...is Gorbage?" I search the room for an idea, but all cleverness has escaped through the cracks in the stone. Nawaritum quickly speaks for me. "I'm sure it looks more impressive written down than it sounds." "It would have to be." Tirigan quips. "Still, you are my guest of honor. You will have a room here in my palace and will write of my most glorious reign. Tonight I will share with you my wonderful plan.

I, the former leader, was finally showered with gifts and treated like a king once more. Though wine and women no longer gauged my worth. I added berries to my water, to make Tirigan believe I had a belly full of wine. I laughed loudly and spoke brashly, once more acting like the barbarian I once was. But this was just a false face I wore, to gain the trust of Tirigan, and spend time with Nawaritum. Once both of us appeared to be full of wine and merriment, Tirigan leads me to his private room. The room was

adorned with pillows and silks, not at all like the room
of a bloodthirsty barbarian.

"Do you know the key to domination,
Gorbage?" Tirigan asks me, as he draws close the
curtains, a bafoon's smile still on his face. Before I
can speak he answers for me. "Expose your weakness,
then attack from that weakness. I've spent the last few
years attacking farmlands and villagers, which has
weakened the strength of gold in the land. We Gutians
don't use gold, so economical downfall means nothing
to us. We have the Akkadian army believing that we
are small armies of weak individuals that can only
attack the defenseless, and our men know only the
victory. Our enemies see us as weak, we see ourselves
as unstoppable, and because of that...we are
unstoppable. We now can show our power. We will
march against the cities of Sumar. We will take all of
the Sumerian lands, and grow as a mighty nation. No
longer will we be barbarians fighting claw and
tooth-like the oafish boar, we will reign over the lands

like eagles. Controlling anything our eyes can see. Once the Akkadians see that we have stopped the most powerful army in the land, they will not fight us. They will beg to join us. They will plead for us to spare them...and we will slaughter them all like pests." With each line, his eyes grew larger and more firey. He spoke like a man driven made with wine. Though I knew that my people would soon be slaughtered at the hands of a much larger and more advanced army, I had little pain in my heart. Unlike the farming village I helped survive, this group arrogantly attack a stronger foe. Like a bee that stings the bear. After a bit more ranting Tirigan let the wine settle in his belly and excused me so that he may sleep.

As I walked the hallways back to my own room, I was stopped by a soft hand reaching through the darkness. I felt it pull me into a side room, a strength that seemed to pull me in by the heart, more than by the arm. Nawaritum had taken me to her private quarters as well. This room also seemed less barbaric than expected. Her walls were covered in books, more than even Enzu had. Her tables were covered in maps, as well as pens and inks as if she had created books herself. "The fool has told you his plan, did he not?" She whispers to me. My eyes still travel from book to book, as I start to wonder how she can intimidate each book better than I could or was she also looking for the secrets? She moved her face to catch eyes with mine again. "Yes, he told me of his plans," I answered. "Though I am a learned woman and his queen, he will not tell me of his plans. He fears that I will turn the people against him. He believes that only his thoughts are truth, and all others are false." I explain Tirigan's plot to march against Sumar. "Goro." She says to me in a sad and timid voice. "Are we still not your people? Are you content in our suffering? Will you really not lead us away from Tirigan's destructive war?" I turn my eyes to her maps. "A leader leads because he is confident in where he goes. Tirigan picks a direction and assumes it must be right, simply because he has picked it. He is no leader. A good leader keeps a map and knows the path ahead. I have no map, I don't know where I am going or what lies ahead. If I lead, I will be no better than Tirigan. Blindly sending my people out to die. Gutians are warriors, and I have no weapons." Nawaritium softly brings my hand to my leather-bound book. "Your knowledge is your weapon, a mind is stronger than steel." I feel shame flow into my face. "I am not intimidating enough to make the books talk to me." Nawaritum's eyes crinkle in confusion. So I open the book and look at it in the way that Enzu would. Nawaritum let out a long laugh.

For the next several nights Nawaritum showed me how to draw lines and squiggles like the ones painted inside each book. She teaches me their names, and how their names change as they stand together, just as a warrior becomes an army as they stand together. I asked if any of her books can save Enzu, but she only shook her head. "Books can take you anywhere, but I have yet to find the book that can take you where your mentor has gone." Still, I could not abandon my search for knowledge, simply because I have had a taste. Once I mastered reading, and writing, I asked to learn more.

. I slowly birthed from the child-like mind of a barbarian to a much more clever thinker. After one of our lessons on philosophy, a guard burst into Nawaritum's room. At first, he was shocked to see another man in the queen's chambers but instantly gained his focus back. "Tirigan's army has marched against Utu-hengal, leader of the Sumerian people. I was asked not to tell you until after he left. Grief struck Nawaritium and me, as it was too late to stop the slaughter about to take place. The next few nights were deathly silent in the palace, as there were no guards execpt Nawaritum's, there were no drunken parties, nobody but the women and the children...just as it had been before. This is how it was for Gutian women, their men out fighting, who will come back if anyone? A constant state of worry and no promise of answers.

A woman that trades goods with the nearby town of Dabrum returned with terrible news. "Trigan blocked the river, trying to block all water from Utu-hengal. He did not take into account Utu-hengal's desert reserve of water. Not only did it not weaken the Sumerian army, it enraged them. Every Gutian man was slashed in twain, expect Tirigan himself, which ran naked and bare-footed to Dabrum. Where he hid with his secret wife and child. But once the people of Dabrum learned that the entire Sumerian army was descending upon them, wanting Tirigan, the people bound him and his second family and delivered them up to Utu-hengal. The people of Dabrum said that they heard Tirigan and his second family scream in torturous agony for two nights before Utu-hengal removed Tirigan's head."

Most women would be ashamed or angry to learn that their husband had a secret second family, but Nawaritium was far more heartbroken for all of the women who just learned of the loss of their husbands and sons. Without warriors, the Gutian people were vulnerable. There was no leader and no army. For barbarians, this meant the end for all. And to the people outside of the Gutian tribe, this marked the end of the Gutian people. In many ways, though, this marked the best moment for them as well.

For the next 20 years, the Gutians lived peacefully in the mountains. Nawaritium served as their queen, the mother of knowledge. She was beloved as if she was each person's birth mother. I

served as her husband, but not her king. As promised,
I would never again lead. I learned from Nawaritum
each day, and we became known as a people that were
clever instead of barbaric.

Chapter 7

Nawaritum started a long-term relationship
with the country of Elam. At one point our old

enemies the Akkadians made a plan to attack the Elam city of Larsa. Larsa sent a message to Nawaritium for aid. "What am I to do?" Nawaritium asked of me. "We are finally a learned people of peace, yet I cannot let the Elamites die," I tell Nawaritum the story of the farmers under attack, and how we can use strategy to defend the defenseless, and still be a people for peace. "Truly my love, you are blessed with a mind unlike any man's!" So we train our strongest and most clever young men to become defenders. To use the layout and the strengths of Elam to our advantage. Sure enough, though Akkadia had the strength and the numbers, we were victorious and survived without a single loss to our ranks. As we returned home the people sang and danced in celebration of their mother Nawaritium. Though she tried to give the credit to me, no one, least of all me, would hear a word of it.

Little did we know that in the town of Mari, in the country of Elam, a meeting was taking place that would change everything forever. At a table sits

Esnuna, timid king of Elam and long friend of
Nawaritium. A dark figure sits opposite him.
"Understand, I could not fight against Akkadia and the
Gutians. If you lose, Elam will be lost in the middle.
We are poets and writers, not warriors." Esnua pleads.
The man across from him leans forward, but still
dressed in the shadow says: "Call upon your mother
protector again, but this time you must ask her to join
you in person. Send her here to Mari, and her troops to
Terqa. We will bring no harm to her, as you request,
but her children will lay down their weapons and serve
us. We will have her tactical mind and our ferocious
warriors. We will be able to take on Sumar and
Babylon at once."

No more than a week passes, and a letter is
sent to Nawaritium, asking that she send troops to
Terqa to defend against a small army. In return,
Esnuna invites her to his palace in Mari for a
celebration. He claims to have new poems written in a
style she is not familiar with. Nawaritium's curiosity

is peaked. However, something does not feel right to me. Why send an army to one place, but her to another? Why would he not come to the Zagros mountains? I share my concerns with Nawaritium, and she offers to send all of the Gutian soldiers to Terqa. "I trust my life to Esnuna, but just in case is mistaken about the number of soldiers marching against him, I will send all of our people, and Terqa is less than a days journey from Mari if anything goes wrong everyone can be there to defend Mari if need be. You will be there to protect me, and our people will have each other. If our kingdoms are to live in peace, we must learn to trust." Nawaritium says as she lays her soft hand against my shoulder in reassurance. Though I am still uneasy with the plan, I trust my love's judgment.

I travel with Nawaritium to Mari. We enter the palace that always smells of fine jasmine and has an abundance of olives to eat. Nawaritium is greeted by Esnuna, and the two immediately speak of art and economy. These are subjects that I've become quite versed in, and despite my charred skin and panther cloak, I usually fit in well in such a society. Though something keeps catching the edges of my eye. Some kind of movement near each doorway and window. I try to play it off as some vulture flapping its wings before I notice them, but the more it happens, the more nervous I get. A loud slam shakes the floor, as the music ceases and Esnuna's face drains of all color. All of the doors are covered by very heavy beams.

"A trap?!" I shout at Esnuna as my hand reaches out for the throat of the quivering king. "No, no I promise" he begs. "Nobody will harm Nawaritium, that was the deal. No bloodshed, it is to be a peaceful end to the war. Look, the Akkadians are telling your people now that the war is over. With you here, Gutians will have no reason to fight, the Akkadians can have our land and yours and nobody has to die. Please believe me, I only wanted to do what I must to save us all."

Nawaritium, Esnuna, and I gathered at the window to watch the end of the war. Though I felt betrayed by our friend, a part of me hoped he was right. After all the Gutians had done to the Akkadians, maybe this is the best way to finally put this all to rest. What happened next was unexpected.

As soon as the Gutian people heard that their mother was kidnapped and that the Elamites had a part in it, the Gutian people split into two groups. One side attacked the Akkadians, while the other slaughtered the Elamites. Even in my time as a barbarian, I had never seen a more savage and bloody site. Each Akkadian and Elamite was not simply killed, they were shredded. This became a massacre. The land became stained red and the smell of death crept up our noses many miles away. Then, just when we thought the worst was over, the two Gutian armies started making their way back. However, with each group covered in blood and gore, no person could recognize the other. In their frenzy and confusion, they turned on each other. Mother's attacked children, husbands killed wives, neighbors and friends slaughtered each other with a rage of madmen.

The end result: the entire Akkadian empire, the Elamite people, and every Gutian….was dead. In mear hours, because of the capture of one woman, three entire groups were erased from history. Esnuna was speechless as he stood frozen in horror as he saw his entire empire crumble before him. Nawaritium, the last of the Gutians, had a cold and solemn look on her face. As if she were one of the books I learned to hold so dear, I read her face clearly. This was the ending to our story. We were no longer barbarians, we were no longer learned people, not kings nor queens, not warriors, not nomads. Everything we thought was important in life was gone in just a few hours. This palace might as well be a cave, as now all coins, all

titles, everything was meaningless. I looked to my love
as she grieved the loss of her people a second and final
time.

Once more I travel the wilderness
without a people, this time, however, I was
not alone. I knew who I was. "Goro…"
Nawaritium began, with tears in her eyes.
"Where do we go now? What is our next
journey?" My rough and scarred hands
gently wipe away her tears as I whisper
"You are my people now. Anywhere I go is
home, so long as we are together."
Together we traveled, sharing our
knowledge and our stories until Nawaritium
fell ill. As I held her and felt her breathing
slowed, I cursed my life. "If only I found the
book that can bring immortality, I could
save you and Enzu." Nawaritium smiled,
not just with her teeth but with her eyes as
well. Those eyes that haunted me from the

first time I saw them. "Your book." She said
weakly. I grab the leather book given to me.
"This?" I ask. "You are speaking through a
fever, this book is blank. See?" I open the
pages again to show her the book that she
knows all-to-well, in hopes of reaching her
mind. But her mind was not gone, as I had
feared. "Write about Enzu, write about me.
Tell your story and we WILL be immortal."
Barely had she finished her last word, she
too closed her eyes and went on to the long
sleep. I spent my remaining years penning
my story, in the book you now hold. I
thought the mind was stronger than steel,
but a mind without a heart is more useless as
a king without his people.

     I heard that Esnuna took his own life. It's a
real shame. I wished for him a long and healthy
life, just like the punishment I had to endure.

www.ingramcontent.com/pod-product-compliance
Lightning Source LLC
Chambersburg PA
CBHW020502160726
47991CB00007B/2772